Everything
and
Nothing

S.L. Freeman

Everything and Nothing

ISBN No. 978-0-6151-8413-5

For anyone who has lost something or someone truly dear to them

The difficulties of life are intended to make us better, not bitter

Mandie Ellingson

Chapter One - The Jacksons and The Actons

January 15, 2006

The blizzard had reached gargantuan proportions. All of New York City was asunder. At least 10 more inches of snow was expected through this Sunday night. In a modest, quaint one-bedroom apartment on 135th Street in Harlem, Shari Jackson stood before the stove, stirring gravy for the mashed potatoes she cooked along with some of her infamous meat loaf for her and her husband, Tony. Both Shari and Tony were white-collar professionals. But nobody would have to go to work on Monday, so it was an impromptu 'movie night.'

Tony set up the DVD player in the living room. He prepared a double feature, a comedy film and a horror flick, Shari's two favorites. The TV program that was on at the time was interrupted by a special news bulletin. All roads, hospitals, businesses, churches, and every-thing else, were closed. The good Lord had made his own curfew for everyone, Shari thought to herself. Tony's stomach was growling. But the sounds of crashing aluminum broke up the routine.

"My water broke!" Shari's yell could be heard a mile away. Tony ran into the kitchen in a panic.

"Oh God, well, OK, let's get you to the hospital, I'll get your coat, stay right where you are!"

"The hospitals are closed, baby! I am gonna go lie down on the bed." Shari gingerly walked over to the bedroom with Tony's help, a trail of liquid following her.

"I am gonna call Dr. Harris and get some directions." Tony dialed the doctor and explained the situation.

"I'll be right over," Harris said, hanging up immediately.

Dr. Joe Harris, a longtime family friend, knew Tony's parents from high school. He lived three blocks away. He trudged through the snow and arrived in 45 minutes to Jackson's apartment. Meanwhile, Tony called all of the family members to let them know Shari had gone into labor and that the doctor was on his way. With the weather the way it was, a certain excitement flooded the air for the entire Jackson clan. Several family and friends braved the elements and walked in the storm over to the apartment.

Dr. Harris performed a quick examination of Shari and knew that it was time to soon deliver a child. He had all of the equipment he needed. Tony was told to bring towels and water and extra pillows. After an hour of contractions, and hand grabbing, and Tony rushing to the door to let anticipating relatives and friends in to sit in the living room and wait, it happened.

Dr. Harris delivered a 6-pound, 3-ounce bundle of joy, a girl, Angela Renee Jackson. The waiting family and friends jumped around like they'd won a million dollars as an exasperated and thrilled Tony emerged from the bedroom with the news.

"Oh God, thank you so much," Tony said, dropping to his knees in tears as the family surrounded him, laughing, crying, and holding cigars up that they had picked up out of a box Tony left on the living room table. Mother and child were doing just fine. Hero of the moment Dr. Harris went home a happy and fulfilled man, having brought unbelievable joy to the Jackson's and the first grandchild for his old friends, Tony's folks, Mary and Johnny Jackson.

Law abiding, solid, happy, fun-loving, determined, and hard-working people, the Jacksons felt blessed beyond belief.

Life had given them everything they ever wanted.

February 25, 2006

Ray Acton woke up feeling fortunate. He was about to leave prison after a six-month stretch for armed robbery. He did the crime, he did the time. He pleaded guilty in court, knowing that the evidence was too much for him to even front like he didn't do it. He did it. But he kept telling himself that he did his time. Walking out with what he walked in with, a watch, a wallet, and a cell phone, plus an additional $100 from the state, Ray went directly to his brother's apartment on 135th Street in Harlem. It was still cold, but the snow was long gone.

Ray's twin brother, Alvin, was there, on the couch smoking blunt and counting money. Alvin was good at counting money. Ray was good at making it for Alvin to count. Ray, who felt he had gotten a new lease on life after he left jail, saw his brother, and knew that he had renewed an old lease instead. The two hugged each other, talked about a few people both of them knew who were still in the joint, and then got back to business…the dealing business.

The Acton brothers had a rough upbringing. Their parents died when they were teenagers and left them no guidance and no authority figures. They ran wild, robbing and assaulting and dealing drugs for a strong, five-year period while living in and out of group homes. They made thousands and thousands of dollars, yet never used the money to do anything other than buy more drugs to sell and get a luxury car for each of them. They never sold a drug below 125th Street.

Alvin finished counting the money and went outside on the stoop. Willie Cranston was walking up 135th Street looking angry. About 200 feet from Alvin, Willie reached into his waistband for a gun. Alvin noticed him at about 150 feet and pulled his out. Willie got 20 feet away and started yelling.

"What the hell were you doing on my block yesterday, man?"

"That ain't your block no more, it's my block. You let it go, and now other cats came in and they're working it now, so step back homey."

Chapter Two - The Tragedy

Shari and Tony sat at the kitchen table, feeding little Angela her baby food and watching her giggle and ogle the room. Angela was a happy child, always laughing and behaving like an adult. She went to sleep on time, she never woke up angry in the middle of the night, she was a wonderful baby. She was pleased to meet everyone she encountered, and her grandparents were on their way over to visit, yet again, and spoil her rotten. Shari's parents, who live in Aruba, were to fly in to New York the next day for their first meeting with their first grandchild.

The first shot startled both parents. Tony got up.

"What the hell was that?"

"I don't know but close the window, hun. This hasn't happened in a while around here."

The second shot sounded just like the first, coming only a few seconds later. Everyone had ducked down and Shari grabbed Angela. Tony was under the windowsill. Shari looked at Angela to see if she was OK. She noticed a small dot on her forehead. Angela's eyes were half open, staring straight at her mother. Shari hadn't even noticed the small pool of blood forming on the floor under and around her arm that was cradling Angela.

"Oh Jesus, Jesus, Jesus!"

"What, baby?" Tony said, rushing over.

Little Angela was dead. Sudden grief and pain were grossly insufficient words to use to describe the next several hours of Shari and Tony's life. The screams they let out were heard a block away. It took the police 12 minutes to pry the baby from her parents' arms. Willie was dead on the sidewalk directly across the street from the Jacksons' apartment. Alvin was in the back of the police car, arrested for the murders of both Willie Cranston and little Angela Jackson. Ray stood in the vestibule, stunned. The lease was already up.

For the Jacksons, it was different, but it wasn't. Shari had been told by Dr. Harris that she wouldn't be able to have any more kids because of a problem with her ovaries found after Angela's birth. She and Tony didn't care. They had only planned to have one child, and the diagnosis, to them both, was God's way of saying that they needed to only nurture the one child as well as they could. God never gives you more than you can handle, Shari had always believed. This was no longer the case. Shari and Tony never got over their loss. Ever. Nothing got them out of their misery or lack of faith over the next five decades; not family, not friends, not Alvin's future conviction, not therapy, not money, nothing. They lost their jobs and became homeless, riding the subways of New York City and begging for food and shelter 24 hours a day.

On the day of Angela's birth 50 years later, Shari and Tony killed themselves with an overdose of pills they stole at age 75.

As it turned out, life gave the Jacksons everything...........

S.L. Freeman

Everything and Nothing

S.L. Freeman

Everything and Nothing

S.L. Freeman

Everything and Nothing

S.L. Freeman

Everything and Nothing

S.L. Freeman

Everything and Nothing

S.L. Freeman

Everything and Nothing

S.L. Freeman

Everything and Nothing

S.L. Freeman

Everything and Nothing

S.L. Freeman

Everything and Nothing

S.L. Freeman

Everything and Nothing

S.L. Freeman

Everything and Nothing

S.L. Freeman

Everything and Nothing

S.L. Freeman

Everything and Nothing

S.L. Freeman

Everything and Nothing

S.L. Freeman

Everything and Nothing

S.L. Freeman

Everything and Nothing

S.L. Freeman

Everything and Nothing

S.L. Freeman

Everything and Nothing

S.L. Freeman

Everything and Nothing

S.L. Freeman

Everything and Nothing

S.L. Freeman

Everything and Nothing

S.L. Freeman

Everything and Nothing

S.L. Freeman

Everything and Nothing

S.L. Freeman

Everything and Nothing

S.L. Freeman

Everything and Nothing

S.L. Freeman

Everything and Nothing

S.L. Freeman

Everything and Nothing

S.L. Freeman

Everything and Nothing

S.L. Freeman

Everything and Nothing

S.L. Freeman

Everything and Nothing

S.L. Freeman

Everything and Nothing

S.L. Freeman

Everything and Nothing

S.L. Freeman

Everything and Nothing

S.L. Freeman

Everything and Nothing

S.L. Freeman

Everything and Nothing

S.L. Freeman

Everything and Nothing

S.L. Freeman

Everything and Nothing

S.L. Freeman

Everything and Nothing

S.L. Freeman

Everything and Nothing

S.L. Freeman

Everything and Nothing

S.L. Freeman

Everything and Nothing

S.L. Freeman

Everything and Nothing

S.L. Freeman

January 15, 2056

…and nothing.

About the Author

S.L. Freeman was born in New York City in 1966. He's an author, webmaster, and former sportswriter and news reporter at various publications. His first book was *Buzz*, written in 2007. He has lived in New York, New Jersey, Illinois, Texas, and Washington, D.C. He currently lives in New York City.